TRUE BEAUTIFUL GAME

Jon Blake started writing for children in 1981, when he was an English teacher. He has now written over thirty books, including *The Supreme Dream Machine*; *Little Stupendo*, which was shortlisted for the Children's Book Award; and the picture book *You're a Hero, Daley B!* His children's television drama *Life* was shortlisted for a Writers' Guild Award. He has also written several plays for adults and was the Wales winner of the Radio Nations Comedy Cup 2001. Jon taught Creative Writing at the University of Glamorgan for several years. He now lives in Cardiff, visiting schools regularly and teaching community writing courses in the Rhondda.

Books by the same author

Little Stupendo

Little Stupendo Rides Again

Little Stupendo Flies High

The Supreme Dream Machine

First published 2002 by Walker Books Ltd
87 Vauxhall Walk, London SE11 5HJ

2 4 6 8 10 9 7 5 3 1

Text © 2002 Jon Blake
Cover illustration © 2002 Phil Schramm

The right of Jon Blake to be identified as author
of this work has been asserted by him in accordance with the
Copyright, Designs and Patents Act 1988

This book has been typeset in ITC Highlander Book

Printed and bound in Great Britain by The Guernsey Press Co. Ltd

British Library Cataloguing in Publication Data:
a catalogue record for this book is
available from the British Library

ISBN 0-7445-9016-7

TRUE BEAUTIFUL GAME

Chapter One

It's all on the black. Just like the Davis–Taylor final in '85. That, of course, was for the World Championship. This match is for a 50p bet with Kerry Healey. An audience of eighteen million watched the Davis–Taylor final. An audience of seven are watching us.

I line up the shot. The black needs the merest touch on the left side. Should be easy. Then, out of the corner of my eye, I spot a dreaded figure joining the audience. Colin Dobson. C.D. Creeping Death.

Now I'm convinced I'm going to miss.

"Come on, Jamie! You can do it, boy!"

The voice belongs to Rocco, my mate. As usual, he is hyped up. I tell him angrily to shush, then stand away from the shot. I want so much to ignore Creeping Death, but I can't help glancing in his direction. There he is, in his waistcoat and shiny shoes, watching without expression. I don't think I've ever seen Creeping Death express an emotion. Sometimes I wonder if he's human at all.

"Get a move on, Jamie."

It's Kerry. He can see I'm sweating.

I chalk my cue. Creeping Death smooths his hair. Creeping Death's hair is gingery-blond. It sits on his head in tight little waves like a piece of ruffled silk. I've never seen hair like it – on a human.

Ah well. Here goes. Make a firm bridge, cue back, and...

Damn! How did I miss that? How?

Kerry steps up, rolls the black five centimetres into the corner pocket, and holds out his hand for the 50p.

"Jamie!" says Rocco. "You *useless* beggar!" He hammers his head against the wall. I pay up, making the usual excuses.

And then, from behind me, comes a quiet, strangely grating voice. "You've got a problem with your stance."

I wheel round. Creeping Death is looking me in the eyes. He hasn't even got bumfluff yet, but his face wears such a weary expression.

"If I need help, I'll ask for it, thank you," I rasp.

"You do need help," he replies.

I snap. "Yeah? And you know everything, do you? Why don't you take me on then, eh?"

I hear my own words as if someone else is saying them. Then I hear Death agreeing to the match, and me saying it's for a hundred quid, and Rocco going "Whaaa...?" By now everyone in the snooker hall is tuning in. A date is set, a time, a referee. Game on.

"You bloody idiot!" says Rocco, as Creeping Death makes his exit.

"Little twat needs to be taught a lesson," I reply.

"Yeah," says Rocco, "but not by you! Not in a million years! That guy could beat you with one arm tied behind his back!"

I deny this of course, but I know it's true. Creeping Death is far and away the best snooker player of our age. Of course, it does help when your parents have had their loft converted and a full-sized snooker table installed. Darling Colin gets to practise night and day – when he isn't watching his complete collection of World Snooker videos.

Once we asked Creeping Death who his favourite player was. Not Jimmy White. Not Hurricane Higgins. Not even Stephen Hendry. No, Creeping Death's favourite player was – wait for it – Terry Griffiths. He'd modelled his whole game on him. Like some slow, fatal illness, he'd creep round the table, measuring each pot like an undertaker.

No fireworks, no risks, just careful, steady, deadly potting. Make one mistake, he'd be in for his feed, and the game would be over.

Me, I'm a Ronnie O'Sullivan man. Impulsive. Brilliant in spurts, useless the rest of the time. I'm the kind of player the public pays to watch. Especially when I'm going to get my arse kicked to the moon by Creeping Death.

Chapter Two

I walk home with my cue in my hand and the weight of the world on my shoulders. I briefly consider making out the whole thing was a joke, but who would believe that? In any case, Rocco's already opened a book on the match: Creeping Death 1–5, Jamie Fry 66–1.

Of course, there have been many great underdogs in snooker. Look at Joe Johnson – 150–1 when he won the World Title in '86. Or Tony Knowles, unknown when he beat Steve Davis ten–one in the first round in '82. But these were still professional snooker players. They had

10

mastered the basics of the game. They didn't close their eyes and hope for the best, like I do.

A car pulls in beside me and snaps me out of my dream-world. It's a flashy motor – an open-top Beemer. Its driver leans over. He's about forty, in an open shirt, with shades and a bushy moustache.

"Hey! Kiddo!" he calls, in a rasping, hung-over voice.

I don't take kindly to being called Kiddo. "You talking to me?" I ask.

The shades man looks both ways. "I don't see anyone else around," he says.

"What do you want?" I snap.

He leans closer. I swear I can smell whisky on his breath.

"Would you know the way to 38 Hillside Rise?" he asks.

"Yes thanks," I reply.

I expect this answer to throw him, but funny enough, he laughs. "All right, smartarse," he says.

"Now tell me where to find it."

I give him directions. They will take him where he wants ... eventually. Then I watch him drive off, wondering what his game is. Perhaps I should have asked him for a lift. After all, I do live at 38 Hillside Rise.

Chapter Three

I hear the row the moment I turn into our road. Half the neighbours are outside. But it's my mum's voice I can hear, loud and clear. I raise my cue and start to run.

It's all happening in front of our house. The shades man is backing towards his car. Mum's pursuing, stabbing her finger at him. Talk about GBH of the earhole! She is lashing him. He can't get in that car fast enough.

"What's going on?" I yell, but Mum doesn't hear me. She's giving him the dictionary of swear-words from A to Z. Shades man revs up the Beemer and scarpers.

"Get inside!" she says to me, as if I've done something wrong now.

"You all right, Shaz?" asks Fran from 35.

"Yeah, now I've seen the back of him," says Mum.

By now I'm busting to know who this guy is. Insurance salesman? Jehovah's Witness? Tory Party candidate? My heart's thumping like a steam hammer as Mum pushes me into the kitchen. She's pretty worked up too, slamming drawers in search of the fags she gave up last week.

"Who was he?" I ask.

"Don't ask," she snaps.

"I just have," I say.

"Someone I used to know," she replies.

"Oh, come on, Mum!" I go.

Mum gives up looking for the fags and just stands there, humming with anger, tears brimming. "As if I haven't got enough problems," she says, then turns to me with a fierce warning. "If he comes here again, you don't open the door to him. Is that clear?"

"Sure." I shrug. "He's nothing to me."

Mum sniggers bitterly.

"What are you laughing at?" I ask.

"He *is* something to you, Jamie," she says. "He's your dad."

Chapter Four

I go through every emotion in the next twelve hours. Sadness at the years I've spent without a father. Anger that he walked out on us. Joy that he's come back. But I can't deal with it. My head is so messed up it could explode.

I always knew about Dad. I've got vague memories of him, but older people's memories are much clearer. Mum's never got a good word to say about him. According to her, he's the most selfish man who ever lived. But I get a different picture from his old mates. To the guys that drink at The Elephant and Castle, my dad's a legend.

One thing is clear: Dad's lived large. He's drunk, he's fought, he's gambled and he's flirted. Excess is his middle name. People still tell tales of his binges which started in the local and ended up in Aberdeen, or Dublin, or Calais. There's one story that he streaked round Tesco for a ten-quid bet.

Now I want to know more. I feel Mum owes that to me. But asking her questions is like touching a bruise. She's told me how he left, and as far as she's concerned, that's enough.

Then, around lunchtime the next day, the open-top Beemer pulls up outside. The man who is my dad climbs out with a big bouquet of flowers. I duck back behind the curtain as he knocks at the front door. Mum is at work, but I remember her solemn warning.

The knocking goes on, and on, and on. Rat-TAT! Rat-TAT! Rat-TAT! Dad even does that to excess. I stay put till it finally stops. But as the footsteps retreat, I can bear it no longer. I've just got to look out of the window.

It is a fatal move. Just as I look out, Dad looks in. His jaw drops. Obviously he has remembered me from yesterday. He gestures frantically for me to open the door. I close the curtain, heart racing. The knocking starts again and goes on for at least ten minutes. Then, at last, he gives up. The car leaves. I kick a stool across the room in anger and frustration.

Chapter Five

Rocco is getting worried about the big match. "I'm going to lose a fortune on this," he says. "I've taken fifty quid on Death and sweet FA on you."

"Then you're fifty quid up," I reply.

"Yeah, if you win! But you ain't going to win!"

"Yeah, so you keep saying!"

I'm starting to get really ratty. I thwack the cue ball into the pack and scatter it to kingdom come.

"You don't want to break like that against Death," says Rocco. "He'll clean up."

"Just shut up and play," I snap.

We get into the game. I'm soon beating him, but

then I always beat Rocco. Rocco has no sensitive touches and no safety play. He treats every ball like it's his personal enemy.

I've just fluked a red into the side pocket (aiming for the corner) when I hear soft applause behind me. I turn, and find myself face to face with the man who is my dad.

He speaks in a deep, worldly burr. "Like father, like son," he says. "Born under a lucky star."

I'm thrown completely.

"You do know who I am?" he adds.

"Yeah," I mumble. I'm wondering how the hell he found me, then remember he saw me with my cue. There aren't many snooker clubs in town, and only one that allows under-eighteens.

"Carry on," he says. "Don't mind me."

Dad sits back and folds his arms. I address the next ball, wanting desperately to impress him. Needless to say, I'm useless. I couldn't hit a cow with a banjo. Rocco cleans up. I curse myself to hell as he drops to his knees like Cliff Thorburn in '83 – except Thorburn had just made the first televised 147. Rocco's highest break was thirteen.

"You win some, you lose some," says the voice behind me.

"I've *never* lost to him!" I go, sounding about eight years old.

"I'll get you a coffee, son," says Dad.

Dad gestures to me to lead the way. I tell Rocco I'll see him and go over to the canteen. Dad shares a joke with the girl behind the counter, then orders two strong coffees, two massive Chelsea buns and a cone of chips. He sits down opposite me, solid, with big hairy forearms. Then he ladles four spoons of sugar into his tea.

"Live fast, die young," he says, and grins with a mouthful of gaps and gold teeth.

"I was *crap* today," I tell him.

"Yeah," says Dad. "But your mate, he'll never improve. Whereas you, son, have got the magic eye."

Coffee ... cakes ... now flattery. He's certainly doing his best to get round me. I'm determined to resist.

"Glad you're taking an interest," I scoff.

"I've always had an interest in you, Jamie," he replies.

"You've got a funny way of showing it," I quip.

Dad looks me level in the eyes. "Your mum hasn't made it easy," he says.

Again I'm thrown. Has Mum prevented him from seeing me before? She certainly wants to prevent it now!

"You've only heard one side of the story," Dad continues.

I decide to drop this subject. I ask Dad if he plays snooker. That's the cue for a ten-minute monologue. Dad's got a story from every snooker hall in the universe. He's been in the merchant navy, see, and played tables from Bangkok to

22

Vancouver. Never good enough to be a pro, but after six or seven pints, a potter to reckon with.

I tell Dad about the match with Creeping Death. He assures me I'll whip Death's arse because I've got the magic eye, and more to the point, I'm his son.

"But I just don't know enough," I tell him.

Dad lays a big paw on my arm with a grip as intense as a grizzly's. "No worries, son," he says. "I'll train you."

Chapter Six

Next day I meet Dad at the Masters Snooker Club. It's a club for adults, but he's pulled a few tricks and got me entry. Dad's not a man to let a few rules and regulations get in his way.

We set up the balls and I line up to break.

"That's your first problem, Jamie," says Dad. "Stance."

Dad straightens me out. Hands that smell of apples and tobacco guide my shoulders into position. He's not satisfied till I'm rock steady, like a camera tripod.

Now my cueing arm will come through

straight and true.

Almost immediately I start getting results. It helps having the right technique, but it also helps having a parent who shares my interest. Mum tries her best, but if she's honest, the game means nothing to her. Dad, on the other hand, is ardent about it.

"They call football the beautiful game," he says, "but this is the true beautiful game. There's nothing like the crack of the cue ball on the black ... the smooth roll across the baize ... the silent drop into the pocket."

Right on cue, I clip the black into the left corner.

"Very nice," says Dad, "but you're not on a red. If you want to excel at this game, you've got to think at least two shots ahead."

"I haven't got that much control over the cue ball," I tell him.

"It would help if you had a decent cue," says Dad.

"Can't afford it," I reply.

"I'll buy you one tomorrow," says Dad.

I pause over the next shot. All this generosity is starting to touch a raw nerve. "I don't want you spending money on me," I tell him.

"Listen, Jamie," he replies. "I've landed a bet. A big bet. I'm not short of a few bob."

"Give it to Mum then," I say.

"I've been paying your mum maintenance twelve years," says Dad. "It's nearly broken me."

"I didn't know that," I reply.

"No. Well, like I said, you've only heard one side," says Dad.

Chapter Seven

That afternoon, when Mum gets home, I've got questions for her. "Mum," I begin, "you know this man that came round – the man you said was my dad?"

"He *is* your dad," replies Mum, tiredly.

"Shouldn't he be paying you maintenance?" I ask.

Mum puts the kettle on and seats herself at the kitchen table. "He does pay me maintenance," she replies.

So Dad told the truth! "Isn't that meant to be for me?" I ask.

"It's for your upkeep, yes," says Mum.

"Shouldn't I get some then?" I ask.

The kettle starts to come to the boil, and so does Mum. "What do you think I buy your food with?" she says. "What do you think I pay your phone bill with?"

"I know, Mum, but I'm nearly sixteen," I plead. "I've got other things I need to pay for. I've got a big match coming up, and I've got to practise—"

"Jamie," says Mum. "We've got to eat! We've got to pay the rent!"

"Rent shouldn't come out of my money," I reply.

Mum boils over. "I've kept you for fifteen years!" she rails. "I've sacrificed *everything* for you! What kind of life do I have?"

"But—" I begin.

"No buts!" says Mum. "I fought tooth and nail for that money! It took me five years to find the bastard!"

I look Mum square in the eyes. Is this true, or is she painting things worse than they were? It's getting so hard to know who to believe.

Chapter Eight

Dad's got a storming great bruise on his cheek when I meet him the next day. "You should have seen the other guy," he says.

"What happened?" I ask.

"I was out with the boys," he says. "Being a bit rowdy, you know, but not causing any harm. Some guy comes up and accuses me of eyeing up his missus. Bit of pushing and shoving, then he clocks me one. So I give him one back."

Dad smiles and knocks back a carton of orange juice.

"What happened then?" I ask, eagerly.

"Someone called the ambulance," says Dad, then laughs like a drain.

"Were you really looking at his wife?" I ask.

"What do you think?" says Dad and laughs even more. "Tell you what – she wasn't half bad. Shame she went off down the hossie – I was going to ask her out."

I'm beginning to understand why my dad's such a legend with the boys. Life's there for the taking for Dad, and it's starting to rub off. As we get down to practice, I'm so much more positive. The doubts have gone.

It's an excellent session. We work on cue ball control – stunning, left- and right-hand side, that kind of thing. At the end of two hours I'm stunning with side – just like the pros. It's like the ball's on a piece of elastic.

"Think what I'll do with a decent cue," I say.

"Come on then," says Dad. "Let's go get one."

Chapter Nine

The Snooker Superstore is snooker heaven. I wander through the array of cues and tables in a warm daze. I want it all, but a twelve-foot slate-bed Corinthian table will set us back three and a half grand. The prices of the best cues are almost as frightening.

Nothing, however, frightens Dad. "Choose the one you want," he says, handing me a nice maple cue to try for size.

"Are you sure?" I ask him.

"Money," says Dad, "is for spending."

I test the feel of a few cues. A salesman comes

over and starts giving us the patter. He recommends a nice cue for a beginner.

"My son's no beginner," says Dad.

The salesman checks the bruise on Dad's cheek and offers us a two-piece hand-crafted ash cue with hand-spliced ebony butt. It looks beautiful and it feels beautiful. The balance is perfect. A chimpanzee could pot with it.

"Do you want it?" asks Dad.

"It's expensive," I remark.

Dad flicks open his wallet and hands the salesman a Visa card. "We'll take it," he says.

Chapter Ten

I walk out of that shop feeling like a prince. We go straight back to the Masters Club, because there's no way I can wait to use my new cue. Dad loves that about me – the fact I'm impulsive, like Higgins. Hurricane Higgins that is, not John Higgins. John Higgins could never equal the best of the Hurricane. You've got to have passion to play like the Hurricane.

"That's the difference between me and Creeping Death," I say.

"That's why you're going to roast him," says Dad.

I'm really starting to believe it now. With this

new cue in my hand, I'm a fifty per cent better player. I take on some long pots and just know I'm going to get them. The balls crack into the pockets like they've been shot from a rifle.

"That's my boy!" says Dad. His face is full of glee as he grabs me by the shoulders and shakes me like a piggy bank. "Now let's burn some rubber!"

The sun is blazing outside. Dad lowers the top of his Beemer, revs up and squeals out of the car park. Springsteen blares out from the stereo with a pumping bass that comes right up your spine. We speed through town getting envious glances and angry horns. Dad has a range of hand signals to deal with these.

Town's soon far away. We pass the industrial estate and the wildfowl reserve and finally reach the old airfield. Dad bumps across a bit of country-side and lands us on the tarmac. Then he stops and gets out of the car. "Your turn," he says.

"Eh?" I gasp. "I can't drive!"

"Now's the time to learn," he replies.

I ease over into the driver's seat. Dad gets in on the passenger side. He runs through the basics while I sit there quietly panicking. But half an hour later I am driving the thing, really driving it! Sure, there's some bumps and stops and gear-crunching, but I'm actually amazingly good. I even get it up to fourth and over fifty miles an hour. By the time I've finished I'm high as a kite.

"That was wicked!" I sigh.

"You see, son?" he says. "You can do anything!"

Suddenly a wave of emotion comes over me. "Why did you have to go away?" I plead.

Dad gets serious. "Sometimes in life," he says, "it's better to do the hard thing."

"How do you mean?" I ask.

"I would have been a terrible father," says Dad. "I was miserable. Hell to live with. I felt like a caged animal." Suddenly he becomes passionate. "I've got to be myself, Jamie! I've got to be! Your mum was turning me into something else – a domestic pet. Women do that, Jamie. They love you because you're a man, then they destroy the thing they love."

I nod, feeling this must be true. My mind replays that scene in *Rebel Without a Cause* when James Dean sees his dad in a pinny.

"I always knew I'd make it up to you, Jamie," adds Dad, ruffling my hair.

Chapter Eleven

The practice sessions get better. I work on building breaks – not just fifteen or sixteen, but twenty, twenty-five, even thirty. I practise safety play and escapes from snookers. We adjust my cue grip and improve my bridge. I'm feeling more and more in control of what I do.

No one else knows what's going on. Rocco's still taking the bets on Creeping Death – his price has shortened to 1–7. I'm still there at 66–1, so Dad gives me twenty quid to put on myself.

"At least that's twenty I'll make," says Rocco.

"Or one thousand, three hundred and twenty

you'll lose," I quip.

"Like I said," replies Rocco, "at least that's twenty I'll make."

Creeping Death is playing on a nearby table. I watch him for a while. He ghosts slowly around the table with the spider in his hand, planning a difficult pot to the far corner. Five minutes later, he slowly screws on his extension. Ten minutes later, his dull but deadly eyes are finally focused on the shot. The ball rolls slowly and surely into the pocket. Death expresses no emotion and moves on to the next shot.

A week ago I'd have been fazed. Now I think to myself, *Must practise more shots using the rest.*

Chapter Twelve

I go for a little jog later that day, to get my fitness up. When I get back, Mum is standing in the living-room. She is holding my new cue.

"Where did this come from?" she asks.

"That's mine," I blurt, taken aback.

"I want to know where it came from," says Mum.

The adrenaline starts to pump. "You shouldn't have been in my room," I reply.

"I have to go in your room," says Mum. "You've got half the mugs in the house in there."

Mum waits.

"I bought a new cue," I tell her. "So what?"

"You can't afford a cue like this," says Mum.

"How do you know what cues cost?" I sneer.

"How do I know?" asks Mum. "Cos I've been saving up to buy you one, if you must know!"

That takes the wind right out of my sails. "I borrowed the money," I mutter. It doesn't sound convincing.

"Have you been seeing your father?" asks Mum, gravely.

"Why do you say that?" I reply.

"I know the way he works," says Mum.

I pause. It's fatal. Mum moves closer. "You have, haven't you?" she snaps.

"Might have," I mutter.

Mum goes mental. "I told you not to see that man!" she yells. "I told you, and you defied me!"

By now my hands are shaking. "He's my father!" I blare. "He's my bloody father, and if I want to see him, I'll see him!"

"Don't you dare swear at me!" shrieks Mum.

"You think you can tell me what to do but you can't!" I shout. "I'm fifteen years old!"

"Yes!" screams Mum, tapping furiously on her own breastbone. "And I'm the reason you've got to fifteen! Not that selfish bastard!"

"You stopped him seeing me!" I bellow.

"What's he told you?" yells Mum.

"Oh, a lot of things." I smirk.

"And you trust him over me?" bawls Mum.

"I like him," I reply, defiantly.

Mum stares in blind anger, chest heaving. She thrusts the cue into my hand. "You take this back to him," she says, in a trembling voice, "and you tell him he's seen you for the last time."

I snatch the cue back and hold it close. "Not doing that," I reply.

"While you live in my house," warns Mum, "you do as I tell you."

"Right," I reply, marching from the room.

The next ten minutes are a blur. I pack frantically

41

as Mum hammers desperately at the door. We struggle in the hallway, blindly, her face red with tears and fury. I escape into the rain with night falling and no clue where to run.

Chapter Thirteen

It is fast turning into a foul night. I'm wearing train-ers, which are soon sodden, and a fleece, which is no better. I arrive at The Elephant and Castle like a drowned rat. All eyes turn on me as I march into the warm, smoky room. I search one way, then the other, but no sign of Dad.

"Anyone seen Keith Fry?" I ask.

I look round at a sea of suspicious faces. "Who wants him?" someone asks.

"His son," I reply.

A head pokes round the corner. It's Dave Lewis, one of our neighbours. "Oh, it's Jamie!" he says.

"It's OK, boys," he tells the others. "What do you want with your dad, Jamie?" he asks me.

"I need to see him," I reply.

Dave's a bit wary. He beckons me over. "I'll tell you where he is," he says softly, "but don't go spreading it around. And don't tell him who told you."

"OK," I reply.

"You'll find him down at Clifftops," says Dave.

"Clifftops?" I reply. "The holiday park?"

"He's got a chalet down there," confirms Dave.

I stare back at him, trying to take this in.

"Are you all right?" he asks.

"Yeah," I mutter. "Thanks."

Back into the wild night, down to a windswept bus station – just a couple of alkies and a kissing couple. I wait ten, maybe fifteen, minutes, then board the 93 to Sudley Bay. It's a long journey. I clutch my rain-soaked cue case to my stomach as the familiar landmarks come and go. Then we're out in the wilds with nothing but speeding cars for company. I climb off beneath the sign that says CLIFFTOPS HOLIDAY PARK – FUN FOR ALL THE FAMILY.

Chapter Fourteen

I knock for several minutes. Eventually the letter-box opens and a pair of eyes stare out. The door opens. Dad stands there in a dressing-gown, looking well rough.

"What are you doing here?" he asks, with an anxious frown.

"I've left home," I reply.

Dad seems alarmed. "Where are you going to go?" he asks.

"Here," I reply.

"Um," says Dad, "that could be difficult."

I ask if I can come in and he backs aside. There

46

is a baseball bat resting by the door. Dad notices my glance at it.

"Had a few threats," he says. "Nothing serious."

"What threats?" I ask.

"That idiot I clocked," replies Dad. "He's got a few pals."

I walk into the chalet. There is a stink of after-shave, stale beer and rotten food. The sides are chock-a-block with pizza boxes, paper plates and empty cans of lager. I don't even realize it's the kitchen till I spot a cooker beneath a cardboard box of videos.

"This is all temporary," says Dad, waving a dismissive hand. "Soon as I'm sorted, I'll get myself a flat and a cleaner."

We go through to the lounge. Posters of naked girls on motorbikes adorn the walls. There is a stereo, a TV-video and a Bullworker in a sea of tapes and CDs. There's also a games console, but it looks as if Dad has either slept on it or flung

47

it against a wall.

Dad kicks things this way and that and offers me an armchair. He doesn't seem to notice that I'm soaked to the skin.

"You've had a row with your mother, have you?" he says.

"She found my cue," I reply. "She knows I've been seeing you."

"You've got every right to see me," says Dad.

"That's what I told her," I reply.

Dad nods. "Good," he says.

I feel a warm glow. Yes, I was right to stand my ground!

"So," I continue, "is it all right for me to stay?"

Dad chews it over. "How are you going to get to school tomorrow?" he asks.

"It's August, Dad!" I reply. "No school in August."

"Right," says Dad.

Long pause.

"So?" I ask again.

"How long were you thinking of?" asks Dad.

"Haven't thought about it," I reply.

"Always think two shots ahead," he quips.

"Like you, Dad?" I say, all matey.

Dad doesn't laugh. "I think you might find it difficult to cope with my lifestyle," he says.

"I'll manage," I reply.

"Besides," says Dad, "this is my office."

I look around. "It is?"

I've never asked Dad what exactly he does. I know it's something to do with buying and selling. I decide now is not the time for further explanation.

"Let's just see how it goes," I suggest.

Dad shrugs. "Sure," he says. "You know me – easy come, easy go."

I smile wryly.

Chapter Fifteen

I phone Mum later that evening. She goes totally mad at me. In a way I'm pleased about this, because it stops me feeling guilty. I tell her I'm fine and not to try to trace me. She rants on and I quietly put the phone down.

I hardly sleep. Dad is snoring like a traction engine in the next room. I'm on the couch with nothing but coats and towels to cover me. My head is playing snooker shots all night, mixed up with memories of the day. I see the row with Mum as a cue ball shattering the pack. I see my moves after leaving home as a long, scrappy break, where I'm always getting out of position. Now and then the face of Creeping Death appears, waiting, waiting for one fatal error.

By morning the hunger is killing me. I stumble round the chalet, searching the boxes for a scrap of pizza. Eventually I uncover a fridge. Inside are four cans of Guinness, a bottle of Worcester sauce, milk which is now yogurt, and a box of eggs. I take out the eggs and look for a frying pan. There isn't one. A saucepan? That neither. How can Dad have eggs, I wonder, without any way of cooking them?

I drop back onto the couch and wait for Dad to get up. It is a long wait. Eventually he emerges, grumpy and silent. He goes to the toilet, where the five pints he quaffed come out of the other end.

"I'm hungry, Dad," I complain.

"Don't start, Jamie," he grunts.

I jump up and fetch the eggs. "Can you show me how to cook these?" I ask.

Dad takes the eggs and studies them as if he's not

quite sure what they are. Then he leads me through to the kitchen area, picks up a pint glass and gives it a quick swill under the tap. He takes the Worcester sauce out of the fridge and opens it. Then he breaks eggs – one, two, three – into the glass. That's followed by a shake of sauce and a frenzied stir with a plastic fork.

Dad offers me the glass.

"No thanks," I reply.

"Suit yourself," says Dad. With that, he tips back his head and sinks the whole golloping load in one, followed by a massive burp.

"Best breakfast in the world!" he rasps, wiping his mouth with the back of his sleeve.

"Is there a shop where I can buy some cornflakes?" I ask.

Chapter Sixteen

When we get to the Masters Club, Herbie, the manager, comes up to us. "The lad's mum's been here," he says.

"What did you tell her?" asks Dad.

"Members only," replies Herbie.

Dad and Herbie exchange a grin. Obviously Dad's briefed Herbie on Mum before. I grin as well, but I'm not really grinning inside. A sick and shaky feeling has come over me.

It's quite a relief to get back to the snooker table. Dad's more relaxed around me once I've got the cue in my hand. We do some more practice on long pots, then some shots off the baulk cushion. As the balls fly my worries vanish. It's another world, a world in itself. You can see why people want to become pros.

"Do you think I'll be a pro one day?" I ask Dad as we drive back.

"If you want it," replies Dad.

"There's an exhibition match at the Arena tonight," I tell him. "John Parrott and Dene O'Kane."

"Sounds good," says Dad.

"Can we go?" I ask.

Dad shakes his head. "Not on a Thursday, son," he says.

"Why?" I ask. "What happens on Thursday?"

"Your dad gets his rocks off," replies Dad.

"Can I come?" I ask.

"In five years' time, maybe," says Dad.

We arrive back at the chalets. It's raining again. All I can see are families cooped up like battery hens, watching telly or playing cards.

"But what am I going to do tonight?" I ask.

"What do you normally do?" says Dad.

"Hang around with my mates," I reply.

"Do that then," says Dad.

"They ain't here," I reply.

Dad turns in his seat and hangs his big hairy forearm over my headrest. "Look, Jamie," he says. "I did tell you I've got my own life. I'm happy to have you stay here, but what you do with yourself in the evenings is your business. Is that clear?"

"But, Dad—"

"No buts."

I sink into a sulk. It's starting to feel a lot more like home.

Chapter Seventeen

But I'm not defeated. I look round at the rubbish tip that is Dad's house and think, *I'm going to clear this mess up*. I go down the shop and get some black bags and all-purpose cleaner. Then I set about the pizza boxes and the paper plates, the plastic spoons and the beer cans. Soon the black bags are bulging and the surfaces are clear.

Next, I attack the dried-on food and the spattered ketchup, the pools of lager and the piles of crumbs. That takes longer, but eventually it's all gone. The chairs are straightened, the rugs are shaken and the bed is made. Clean clothes go on hangers and in drawers – dirty ones in a big card-board box. Finally, I open all the windows, give them a wipe for good measure, and sit back to admire my good work.

It's really quite satisfying getting the house in order. Rather like clearing up on the snooker table. At home I can never be bothered, but here it's different. I imagine Dad's shock and gratitude when he comes home. Then I fall asleep, exhausted, on his bed.

I'm not sure how long I'm asleep. But I'm woken by a blast of heavy rock, full volume, topped off by shouts and screams and laughter. I pull on some jeans, creep to the door and open it.

It's like a scene from a Roman orgy. No, that makes it sound too respectable. The whole room is in chaos, with plates of curry kicked over the floor, couples snogging, and lager flying everywhere. Dad is in his pants, wearing his jeans as a headdress, dancing like a monkey. His legs are going out sideways and his hands are hanging down by the ground. He is blind drunk and singing "Love in an Elevator" at the top of his voice.

Dad's mates are clapping and cheering. Dad lurches around, falls down like a shot horse, then struggles to his feet and sees me.

Oh no, I think to myself.

"Son!" he cries. "It's my little boy!" he adds, to his audience.

"Could you…" I begin.

Dad isn't listening. He staggers over to me, eyes wild, and catches my head under the crook of his arm. Then he's back into his routine, dancing and singing, while I'm trapped there, choking. As he jolts up and down I seriously fear he's going to break my neck. But the crowd is just loving it. One of the women smacks me on the butt. Others whistle and yell and stamp.

At last I get free, red-faced and ashamed. I go straight back into the bedroom, slam the door and jam a table against it.

"Ah, you've upset the poor lamb!" someone
says.

Someone is right.

Chapter Eighteen

The noise goes on till the morning light. Then the door is forced open, Dad staggers in and drops like a boulder onto the bed. I don't think he realizes I'm there. For a while I stay, watching his red face squashed against the pillow, breath like a chemical works. Then he turns over and does an enormous fart. I decide it's time to move.

The state of the chalet is beyond belief. Lager, broken glass and stubbed-out fags litter the floor. Two of the chairs are broken and the walls are splattered with red wine and curry. The whole place reeks of sick – there is a pool on the floor with a skid-mark through it, and another pool in the sink. The toilet floor is covered in piss, which has been walked through into the lounge.

I sit down with my head in my hands. I feel depressed – really depressed. The shaky feeling I got in the Masters Club has come back.

Dad doesn't emerge till the afternoon. I've done nothing till then. He sees me on the couch and frowns. "You been there all night?" he says.

"No, Dad," I reply. "You had a party, remember?"

"Oh, I remember all right!" says Dad.

"Then you should remember waking me up," I say.

Dad shrugs.

"And dancing in your kecks," I add.

Dad chuckles.

"And sticking my head under your arm," I add.

Dad looks at me quizzically. "That," he says, "I don't remember."

"You showed me up good and proper," I tell him.

"Ah, never mind!" says Dad, ruffling my hair. "You teenagers are so self-conscious!"

"Just don't like being made a fool of," I complain.

"Listen to the wild man of snooker!" says Dad.

I pull my head out of reach before he can ruffle my hair again. "And didn't you notice what I'd done?" I ask.

"What's that then?" says Dad.

"Cleaned up the chalet!" I say.

Dad shrugs again. "Jamie," he says. "I was three sheets to the wind last night. Didn't you notice?"

"I spent all evening on it, Dad!" I moan. "I had it perfect! Now look at it!"

I kick a half-chewed naan bread across the floor.

Dad's attitude changes. "Did I ask you to tidy up the chalet?" he asks.

"No," I reply.

"You're starting to sound like your mother," says Dad.

"I only wanted to make it nice!" I plead.

"That's what she used to say!" replies Dad. "You've lived with her too long, son!"

"I never had any choice, did I?" I mutter.

Dad ignores this. "You're a man, son!" he roars. "Not a petty-minded woman!"

He winces and holds his head. "Now look what you've done," he says.

"Do you want a Nurofen?" I ask.

"No!" yells Dad. "I don't want to be looked after, understand? I don't want a wife, or a wet-nurse, or Florence bleeding Nightingale for a son!"

Dad storms into the toilet where there's a crash, followed by five solid minutes of swearing. Then he comes out for another go at me.

"I thought you were a winner, son," he says, "but you're sounding more like a loser every day."

Dad walks out. I feel gutted. Lost, lonely and

gutted. I'm in no shape to take on the biggest match of my life. But the bets have been taken, the tickets have been sold, and the date on them is tomorrow.

Chapter Nineteen

By the time Dad's hangover has worn off, his mood has changed completely. He doesn't actually say sorry, but he buys me a milkshake, tells me a dirty joke and applauds every pot at the practice table. All the same, there's a different feeling between us. The trust has gone.

I'm nervous as hell by the time evening has arrived. Dad buys me a take-away and I think maybe we'll stay in together. But no, he's got a date he fixed up days ago. I want to demand he puts me first but I'm scared there'll be another scene. So off he goes, leaving me to stew.

I don't really sleep. The adrenaline has started to pump and nothing will stop it.

I can't eat breakfast and I can't eat lunch. I watch Dad wolfing down his pie and chips and wonder what it's like to know no fear.

"Aren't you nervous for me?" I ask.

"You'll win," he grunts, but that's what he always says. It no longer means anything to me. I want to feel he's behind me, one hundred per cent. Not just for this match, but for everything – for life.

Chapter Twenty

So here goes. The hall is full and all other games have come to a halt. All my mates are at ringside, drumming on their knees. Two chairs have been set aside, with little tables and glasses of water, just like the World Championship. Leyton Best is referee and Rocco is MC. A perfect job for the lad with the biggest mouth in town.

"Ladies and gentlemen!" he proclaims. "A heavyweight contest over five rounds! First to three wins! Featuring, in the red corner, our very own Jamie Fry!"

Dad nudges me and I walk to my seat. There are

cheers and catcalls. I can't tell if people are for me or just taking the piss.

"And now," continues Rocco, "the Inter-County Under-Sixteen Champion... Creeping Death himself, Colin Dobson!"

The crowd parts. Death moves silently through. I shiver inside as he passes by, then takes his seat, wipes his cue down and stares straight ahead. Again I ask myself, *Why have I put myself through this? Is he* really *the Inter-County Under-Sixteen Champion?*

Leyton tosses a coin. Death calls tails. Tails it is. Death nods towards me to break.

Everything goes wobbly. I glance at Dad. He gives me the thumbs-up. I cue off very gently and the ball doesn't quite reach the pack. There is a groan.

"Foul," says Leyton. "Colin Dobson, four points."

It is the worst start I could have made. I break off again, hit the pack a little too hard, and watch the balls gently part from each other. A perfect set-up for a 147.

Creeping Death rises, coughs softly into the back of his hand, and settles onto his first pot. The red drops safely and surely into the pocket and Death has perfect position on the black. Soon the balls are ticking away like the seconds of my life. From my one mistake, Death makes sixty-five points. The first frame is over.

I glance again at Dad. He's deep in thought. I bluff a smile. He notices and gives me another thumbs-up. Then he's back in thought – about what, I don't know.

Creeping Death breaks. Not perfect, but not bad. One red has come loose over the bottom corner. I've taken on a lot of pots like this in the past week. But that was without the pressure. Now it's a different game altogether.

I try to get the basics right. Stance ... grip ... bridge. One good shot and I'm back in this game.

Crack! It's a good contact. But I miss. I miss by a long way. And the truth is, I knew I was going to.

Creeping Death rises again. He coughs softly into the back of his hand. He settles on a loose red to the opposite corner and in it goes. Then, like some gruesome scavenger, he goes looking for other tit-bits. Not so easy this time. He's always a little out of position. Then he gets a bad kick and the break is over. Only twenty-six.

So. A second chance. An easy red to the centre pocket. At last, a point! But where am I now?

I can't believe I've been so stupid. I haven't thought one shot ahead, let alone two. I'm snookered on all the colours. Unless ... if I can just shave that blue...

"Foul! Dobson, five points!"

I sink back into my chair, so very alone. I do not rise again till Rocco announces a toilet break. Two—nil to Death. I am one frame away from total disgrace.

Chapter Twenty-one

Dad finds me splashing my face with cold water. He appears in the mirror behind me, and for the first time I notice the likeness in our faces. He looks keenly into the reflection of my frightened eyes.

"Come on, Jamie boy!" he says. "He's murdering you!"

"Think I don't know?" I reply.

"You just need to get your head together," says Dad.

"My head's all over the place," I reply.

"You can still do it!" says Dad.

"I can't," I reply.

"Come on, Jamie!" says Dad. "You owe it to yourself! You owe it to me! I want something to remember you by!"

My hands freeze on the taps. "What do you mean?" I ask.

"Never mind," says Dad. "Let's just concentrate on this game."

I turn to face him. "No, Dad," I reply. "I want to know what you mean."

Dad searches for the right words. "I don't think I'm right for this town," he says.

"So you're going," I reply.

"All I wanted," says Dad, "was to make it all right between us."

"You think this is making it all right?" I sneer.

"I do care about you, Jamie," says Dad.

"Well, you don't care enough!" I shout, just as Leyton walks into the toilets.

For a moment there is silence while I stare at Dad and Leyton wonders what the hell is going on.

Then Leyton announces I've got one minute and leaves.

"Come on, Jamie," says Dad. "Let's give 'em hell."

"No!" I yell. "I don't want you here! I don't want to see you ever again!"

"I'm doing what's best," says Dad.

"No you're not!" I yell. "You're doing what suits you! Same as you always do! Now just sod off!"

Dad waits a while, then turns on his heel. When I emerge from the toilets, he's gone.

I take one look at the crowd, the snooker table, Creeping Death waiting, and I walk. I get into the car park and look for the best way to run. But I don't run. I sit on a wall, blind to the world, turmoil running through my veins. One voice in my head screams, "Escape!" But there is another, louder voice. This one says, "Never be a runner! Never be like him!"

I get up and walk back into the snooker hall.

There is total hush as I make my way to the table and prepare to break. Word has obviously got round that something is up.

There is no fear in me now. Snooker, after all, is just a game. I break off like I break in practice – the merest touch on the pack. Beautiful.

Creeping Death comes sniffing. Not one loose red. He goes for the pack and catches it a bit thick.

This time I am the Grim Reaper. Every atom in my body is charged. I begin to pot for real. Red ... black ... red ... black. The pockets are a foot wide. I make a break of thirty-eight and leave the cue ball safe on the baulk cushion. After a few more exchanges, the door opens again. I clinch the frame. Suddenly Death looks beatable, and I've got supporters.

Frame four. A good break-off by Death, and I'm forced to leave him a chance. He makes the pot. This time, however, I don't panic. I know he *is* human, just like Steve Davis was in '85. Sure enough, he catches the jaws of a centre pocket and snookers himself behind the brown. He tries to come off three cushions but blows it. I move in and build myself a winning position. Ten minutes later the frame is mine. It's down to the wire.

You can hear a pin drop as I break. It's Hendry–White in '94. I'm White, of course, except Jimmy's dad was there at every final he played. Jimmy blew that last frame in '94. Some say he choked. But I am too fired up to choke. I've made up my mind – I'm going for everything.

Death builds a break of twenty. I come back with twenty-two. Death's in again for twenty more. I'm back with fifteen. Death makes another ten. With every break he grows more cautious, pondering each pot for a lifetime. But I can't even sit in my chair between breaks.

Death's getting close to the finish line. The cue ball's in the D, the last red has gone, and the yellow's not far from the corner pocket. A long pot would be a risk, but it could seal the frame.

Death ponders, and ponders, and coughs into his hand, and chalks his cue, and ponders some more. He settles into position. He's going for the yellow.

Or is he? He comes up again and glances over at me. He's worried! He's scared to miss!

Death settles again and rolls the cue ball up behind the pink. He catches it a touch too hard and a five-centimetre gap appears between the two balls.

I'm at the table within a second. Yes – the yellow is still on. But I need to swerve the cue ball round the pink – a Hurricane special. I've practised these shots, but it's hit and miss. I could maybe play safe and reach the yellow off the cushion instead.

As if.

I set myself for the shot of a lifetime. The adrenaline is coming like a river. All the pent-up emotion of the past week is behind my cueing arm.

Back it comes, then down on the left-hand side of the ball like a warrior's spear. The ball squirts out like a pip from an orange – round the pink, in a perfect arc, to take the yellow like a dream. The ball drops, the crowd goes mental, and Death views me with disbelief. High as a kite, I set about the other colours. I *know* I will take them.

Green, brown, blue, pink, sweet as a nut. And now, one final, violent release which sends the black smack into the pocket like a bullet train.

The roof comes off. I am the new Hurricane. I've won for the same reason he won. I've got the sixth gear. The passion.

Creeping Death shakes my hand weakly and starts to unload tenners from his wallet. The money means nothing to me. I lay my cue on the table, leave the money and the noise behind me and walk out into a new world.

Chapter Twenty-two

My feet seem to know where they're going. I head past the shops, the churches and the hoardings, and arrive at The Elephant and Castle. I walk straight into the bar, climb onto a stool and call for silence.

Stunned, the regulars cease their chatter. I tell them I've got an important announcement.

"There is something you need to know," I say. "Keith Fry, my father, is not a legend. He is a selfish, pathetic man who has never grown up. And if there's anyone here who admires him, or wants to be like him – you are also pathetic.

Thank you. Goodnight."

I climb down and walk out, feeling so good I could kiss the sky. I begin to run, slowly at first, then faster and faster. I run into my estate, into my road, and only stop when I reach the house I've known all my life. The door is Yale-locked, so I rap on the glass.

After a few seconds Mum appears. There is a moment of shock, then without a word she enfolds me in her arms.

"Sorry," I mumble, but she just hugs me tighter. I cling to her like a monkey – older, wiser and from now on, a winner.